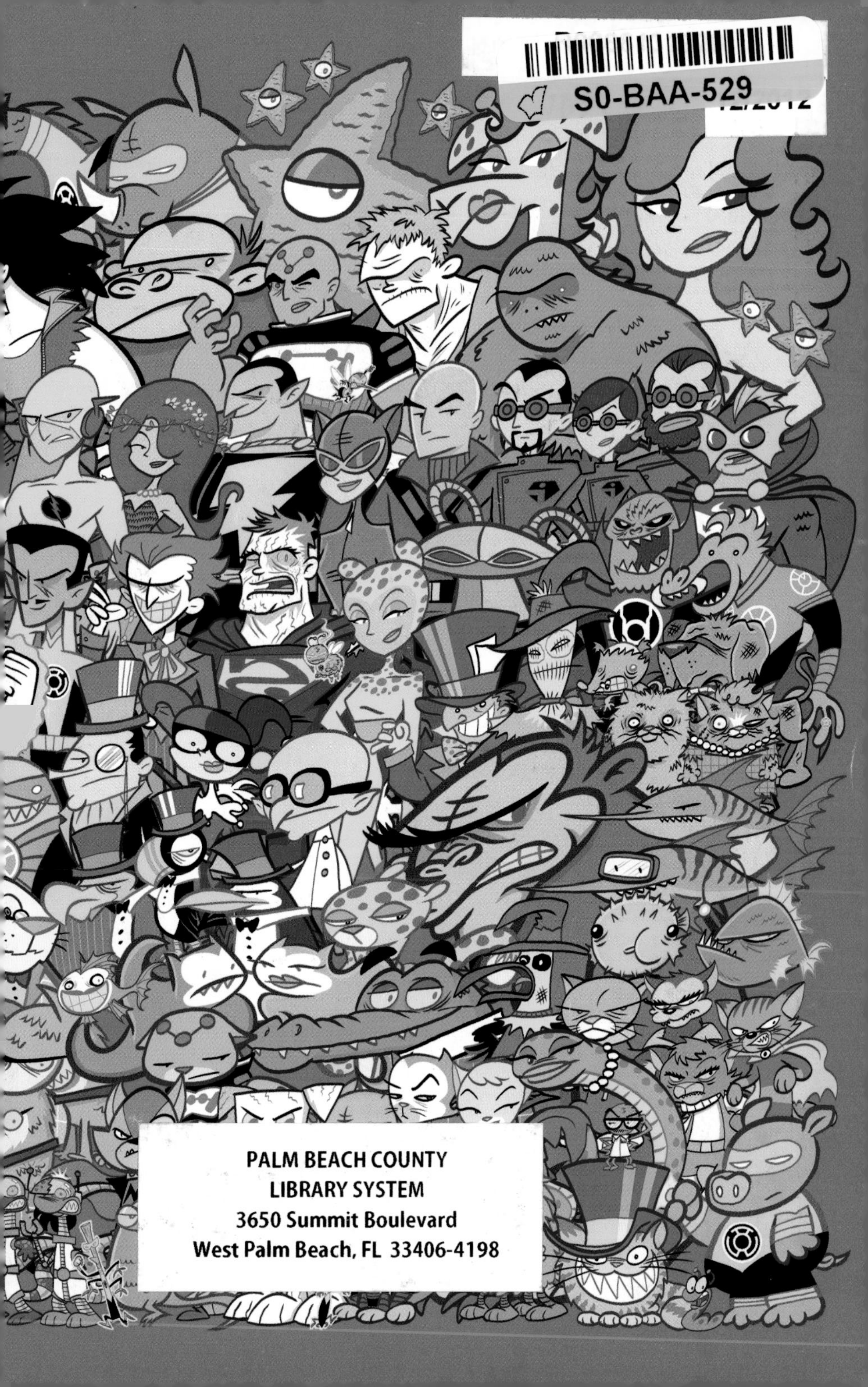

DC™

SUPER-PETS!

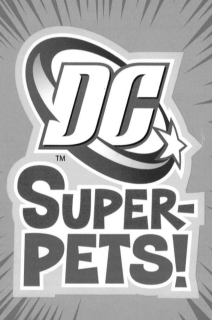

by Steve Korté

THE CAT CRIME CLUB

illustrated by
Art Baltazar

Superman created by
Jerry Siegel and Joe Shuster

Picture Window Books™
a capstone imprint

Starring...

KRYPTO
THE SUPER-DOG!

THE
SPACE CANINE
PATROL AGENTS!

SUPERMAN!

THE CAT
CRIME
CLUB!

TABLE OF CONTENTS!

S.C.P.A. SPACE-COMPUTER

SPACE CANINE PATROL AGENTS

KRYPTO (LEADER)
Powers: Flight, heat vision, X-ray vision, super-speed, super-strength, super-breath

CHAMELEON COLLIE
Power: Shape-shifting

TUSKY HUSKY
Power: Giant tusk

PAW POOCH
Power: Multiple paws

BULL DOG
Power: Horns

TAIL TERRIER
Power: Elastic tail

MAMMOTH MUTT
Power: Hyper-growth

HOT DOG
Power: Fire

Bio: A powerful pack of pooches, the Space Canine Patrol Agents (S.C.P.A.) obey the message of their sacred oath:
"Big dog! Big dog! Bow wow wow! We'll crush evil! Now, now, now!"

Super-Pet Enemy File 012B:
CAT CRIME CLUB

PURRING PETE (LEADER)
Power: Purr-fect plans

KID KITTY
Power: Cat burglary

SCRATCHY TOM
Power: Prowling

GAT-CAT
Power: Hair brawling

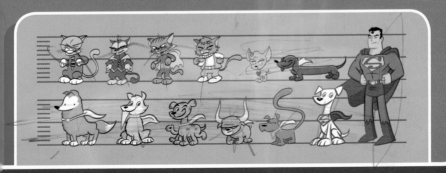

Chapter 1

FETCH!

WOOOOOSH!

Superman soared high above the Arctic Ocean. Flying beside the Man of Steel was his canine crime-fighting companion, **Krypto the Super-Dog.**

"Fetch, boy!" Superman shouted.

The super hero raised his arm. He launched a giant rod of steel into the ocean below. **SPA-LOOSH!**

"Woof!" Krypto barked with delight. The Super-Pet quickly dived into the icy water in search of his toy.

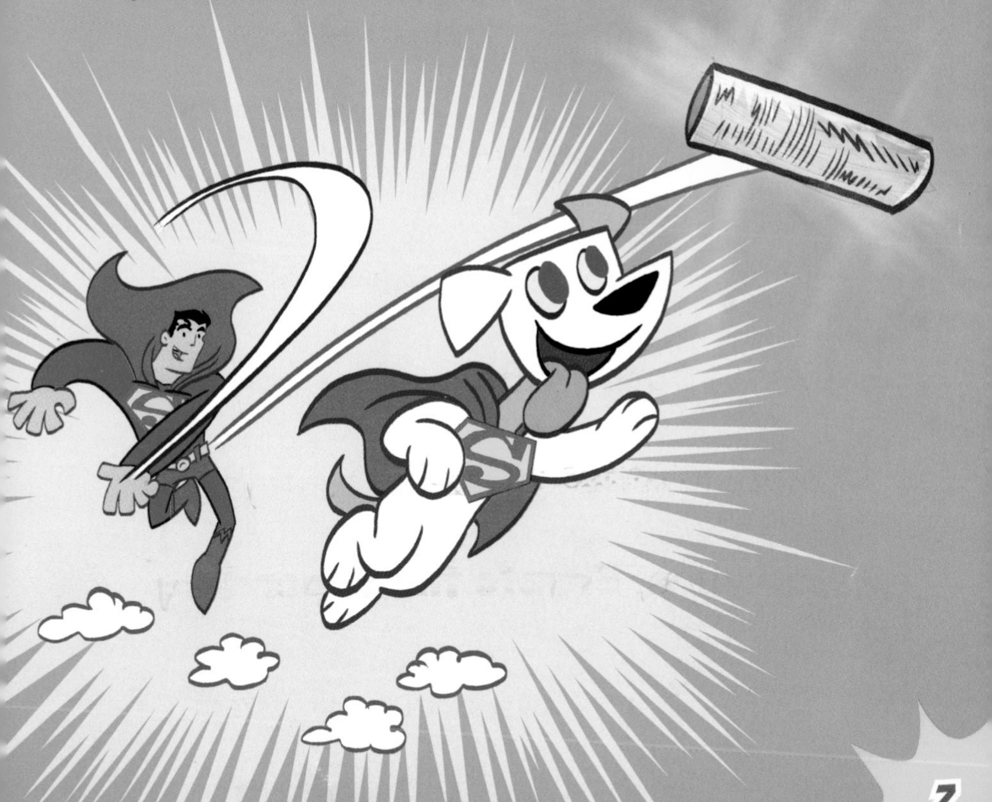

With his X-ray vision, Krypto scanned the seafloor. Superman's powerful pitch had buried the steel rod deep beneath the rocky earth. That was no problem for the Super-Dog.

SCRATCH! SCRATCH! SCRATCH!

Krypto dug at the seafloor with his paws. He snatched the two-ton toy with his super-strong jaws. Then he sped toward the surface. He burst out of the water like a geyser. **FWOOSH!**

Within seconds, Krypto was flying next to Superman again. "Woof! Woof!" the Super-Dog barked.

 **The Man of Steel smiled.** "I guess that was too easy for you," he said with a laugh. Superman grabbed the steel rod from Krypto. He wound up again. "Go deep this time, boy!"

WHOOSH! With all his strength, Superman threw the rod up, up, and away. It sailed into deep space!

ZOOOMM! The Super-Dog sped after the toy. He weaved in and out of asteroids and meteorites.

Then, just as Krypto was about to grasp the rod, a dog-shaped light appeared in front of him. It wasn't a star or a planet. This was a call from the **Space Canine Patrol Agents**. This powerful pack of pooches fought crime throughout the universe.

The shining signal meant that

Krypto should report to the **S.C.P.A.**

headquarters . . . and fast!

"Oh, boy!" Krypto yipped, picking

up speed. "Another exciting adventure

with my furry friends!"

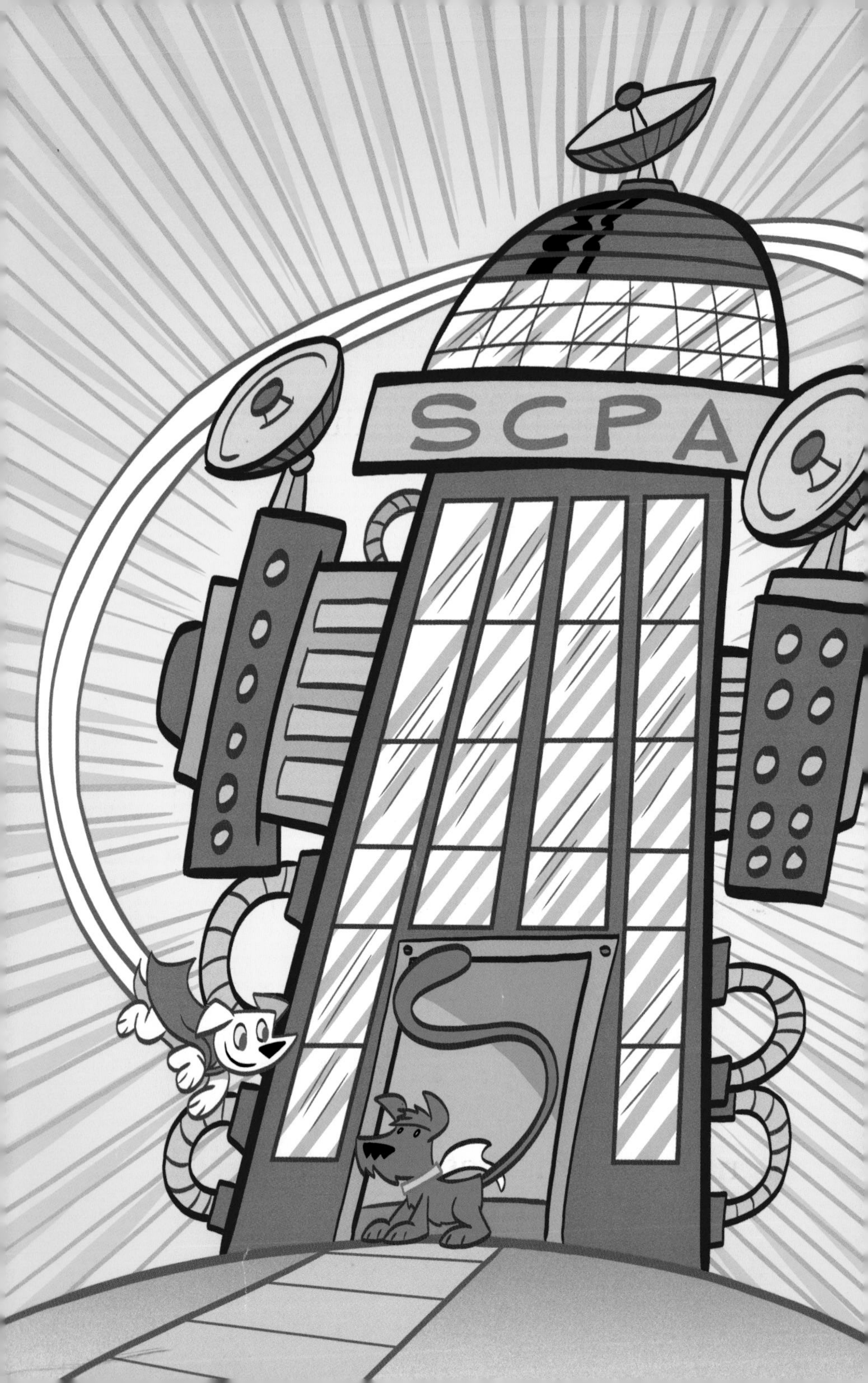
SCPA

Shortly after, the Dog of Steel arrived at the S.C.P.A. Doghouse. **Tail Terrier,** an emerald-colored canine with an extra-long tail, greeted him.

"You're just in time, Krypto," said Tail Terrier. "Today we're testing dogs who wish to join the S.C.P.A."

Krypto followed Tail Terrier to the great hall. There he saw the other members of the S.C.P.A. sitting behind a giant table. **BAM! BAM!** Tail Terrier used his elastic tail to swing a gavel and start the meeting.

The first order of business was to
repeat the oath of the Space Canine
Patrol Agents. Together, all the dogs
said the powerful pledge: **"Big dog!**
Big dog! Bow, wow, wow! We'll crush
evil! Now, now, now!"

TAIL TERRIER

CHAMELEON COLLIE

HOT DOG

PAW POOCH

"The first canine who wishes to join the S.C.P.A. is a poodle named Frenchy," announced Tail Terrier. "What is your special power?" he asked as the pink pooch tiptoed up to the bench.

 **"I can change into a cat!"**

answered Frenchy with pride.

The pooches behind the table were

amazed. Cats were the most dreaded

enemies of the S.C.P.A. There was even

a group of feline felons called the Cat

Crime Club. Why would any canine

want to turn into a cat?

"I would be a perfect spy among the

cat-crooks," said Frenchy, raising his

front paws in the air. With a mighty

POOF and a cloud of pink smoke,

he changed into a Persian cat.

In his right paw Frenchy held a
mechanical mouse, which he dropped
on the floor. **"RRRRRRROWR!"**

Frenchy jumped on the toy. He
grabbed it between his front paws.

Then he kicked it with his rear paws.

"That's just like a cat," said Tail Terrier with a sad shake of his head. "But let's see how you react to catnip." As he spoke, Tail Terrier sprinkled catnip over Frenchy's head.

"Wow!" said Frenchy with delight, as he rolled on the floor and hiccupped. Much to the disgust of the dogs, Frenchy even started purring!

 "Your application is rejected," said Tail Terrier. "You are unable to resist catnip. You're too much like a cat to earn our trust!"

Frenchy sadly slunk out of the room, his tail between his legs.

"The next order of business is tomorrow's All-Paws Circus," said Tail Terrier. "It's the only event where cats and dogs come together in friendship."

"The All-Paws Circus will raise money for the S.C.P.A.," Tail Terrier added. "Krypto has been chosen to guard it all."

As the other dogs cheered, they didn't know that someone was spying on their meeting. In a distant galaxy, members of the evil **Cat Crime Club** were gathered around a radio. They listened in on the S.C.P.A. meeting.

**"Our spy, Frenchy, did a purrrfect job,"** said **Purring Pete,** the Cat Crime Club leader.

Purring Pete let out an evil laugh. "Those dumb dogs didn't suspect that Frenchy's mouse was a radio transmitter," he said. "After we take our catnaps, we'll cat-*nab* the money from the All-Paws Circus!"

Chapter 2

CLEVER CATS

The next day on the Canine-Feline
World, pooches and pussycats arrived
for the All-Paws Circus. The crowds
cheered inside the main tent as the
Space Canine Patrol Agents gathered
to show off their superpowers and raise
money for the agency.

In the ring, **Chameleon Collie** used his shape-shifting powers to change into a horse. Tail Terrier rode on top of him. As they galloped around the arena, Tail Terrier used his tail to lasso the giant horns of **Bull Dog.**

For the next act, Hot Dog perched

on the end of Tusky Husky's giant tusk.

Hot Dog created a giant ring of fire

and did acrobatic flips through the

flames.

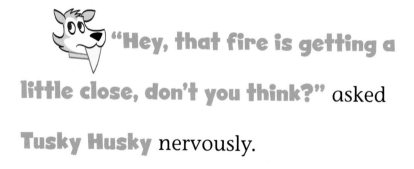"Hey, that fire is getting a

little close, don't you think?" asked

Tusky Husky nervously.

"Don't be such a scaredy-dog!"

answered Hot Dog as he spun through

the air.

For the last act, **Paw Pooch** did an amazing juggling act. He bent his body like a centipede and tossed six beach balls with his extra paws.

FWIP! FWIP! FWIP!

While the canines were busy performing, Cat Crime Club members hid beneath the stands, planning their caper. With an evil grin, Purring Pete called **Kid Kitty** over to him.

"We're going to dress you up as a hot-dog seller," said Purring Pete. "You need to convince Krypto to eat a hot dog that's been flavored with **Red Kryptonite!**"

The kitty criminals knew that Kryptonite came from the Super-Dog's home planet of Krypton.

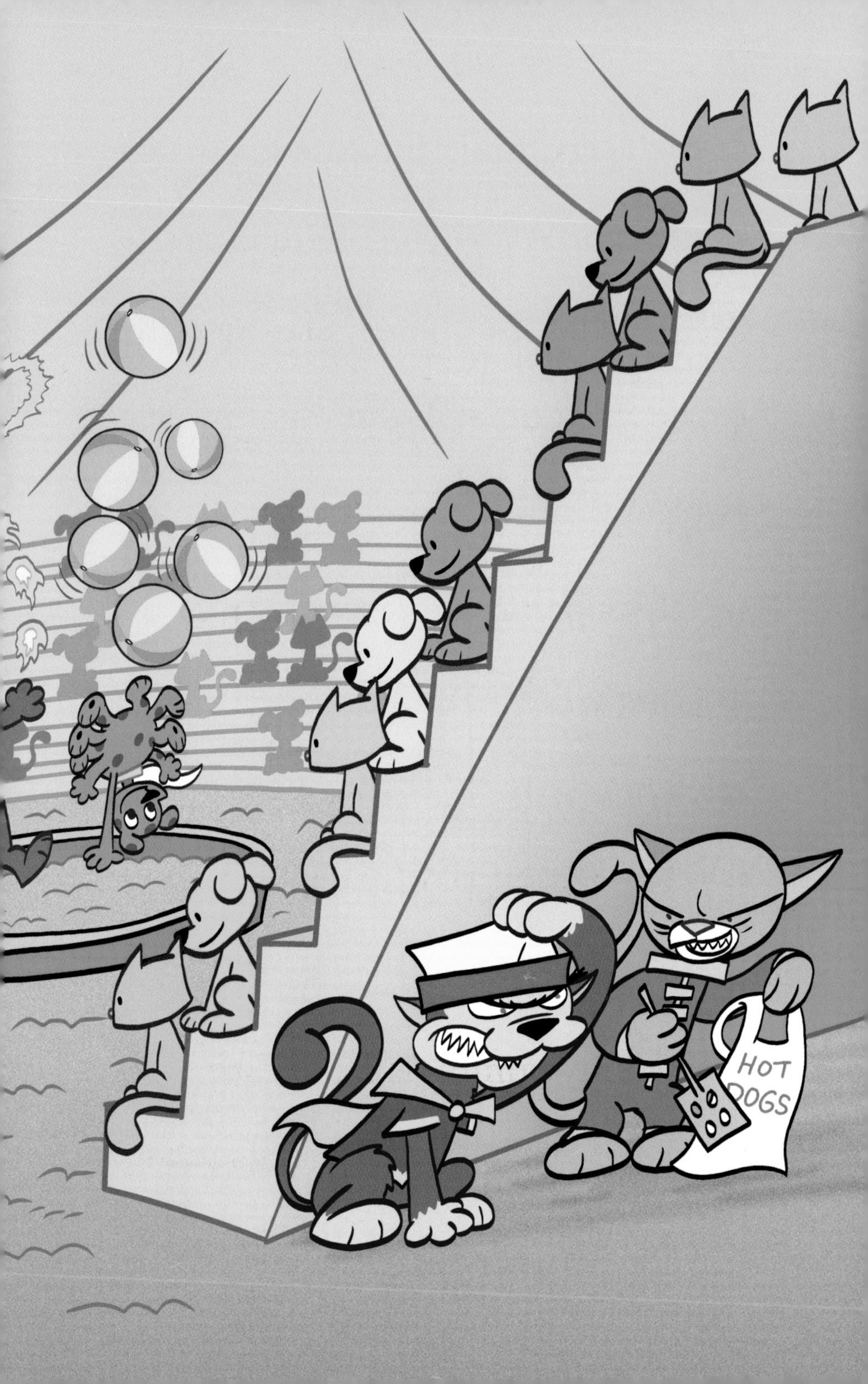
HOT DOGS

The Cat Crime Club also knew Red Kryptonite always had strange effects on the Super-Dog.

"Hey, Krypto!" said the disguised Kid Kitty. "Have a free hot dog with our secret-recipe red catsup!"

Taking a break from guarding the box office, Krypto happily gobbled down the wiener. At the same time, Purring Pete and the other members of the Cat Crime Club broke into the box office. The kitty crooks started stuffing all the money into a giant bag.

"GRRRROWL!" Krypto suddenly spotted them. He sprang into action. "Those plundering pussycats aren't going to get away with this crime!" Krypto said. He leaped into the air, launching himself right at the cats.

FWOOOOSH!

Much to his amazement, the Super-Dog flew right *through* the cats. Krypto landed on the ground with a thud.

WHUMP!

The Red Kryptonite had turned him into a ghost. **He passed right through solid objects!**

Krypto tried to grab the bag of money with his teeth, but he couldn't hold onto it with his ghost-like jaws. He couldn't even bark to alert the other S.C.P.A. members.

"It looks like the circus has a new act named Krypto the Klown!" sneered Purring Pete. The other cat burglars laughed as they ran away with the cash.

* * *

Later that day, after the effects of the Red Kryptonite had worn off, Krypto hung his head in shame at the Space Canine Patrol Agents headquarters. The Cat Crime Club had stolen all the money. The Super-Dog had been powerless to stop them.

Tail Terrier gathered together the other members of the S.C.P.A. in the great hall. He announced that Krypto would be punished for a month.

"You must also return your cape and collar," said Tail Terrier.

How terrible! thought Krypto as he unbuckled his collar. Then he had an even more awful thought: *How will I explain this to Superman?*

Chapter 3

DOG OF STEEL

The canine heroes sadly filed out of the great hall after Krypto had removed his cape and collar. The Super-Dog placed the items on the table next to Frenchy's mechanical mouse. Then, something surprising happened . . .

ZRRT! A giant spark jumped from Krypto's collar to the robotic rodent.

That's odd, thought Krypto. He used his X-ray vision to look inside the mouse. The Super-Dog was amazed to see that the mouse was really a radio transmitter!

Suddenly, he realized that the Cat Crime Club had been spying on the Space Canine Patrol Agents. That's how the pussycats had gotten away with their circus crime.

 Krypto had a plan of his own, though. Knowing that the evil felines were probably listening on the radio, Krypto called out to his fellow S.C.P.A. members: "I forgot to tell you that on my way back from the circus, I saw a planet just beyond Asteroid Alley with a pile of delicious bones."

Krypto held back a laugh. "But the planet had a double red sun," he said, "so naturally I steered clear of it."

The Cat Crime Club was listening to every word. They also knew that Krypto would lose his superpowers under a red sun.

 **"What do you say, fellow felines?"** asked Purring Pete. "Are you up for one more caper before we nap? Let's travel to this planet and grab the bones before those horrible hounds can get their slobbering snouts on them."

The Cat Crime Club piloted their spaceship to the planet just beyond Asteroid Alley. Sure enough, they saw two giant red suns high above. On the planet was a collection of bones, just as the Super-Dog had described. The cats were surprised to see that Krypto was standing guard.

"He's even dumber than we thought," said Purring Pete. His whiskers twitched with delight. "Without his superpowers, how can he stop us? **Let's blast him!**"

Purring Pete pushed a red button
on the control panel. Three giant laser
blasts shot out from the spaceship,
heading right at Krypto! The cats fell
to the floor in laughter.

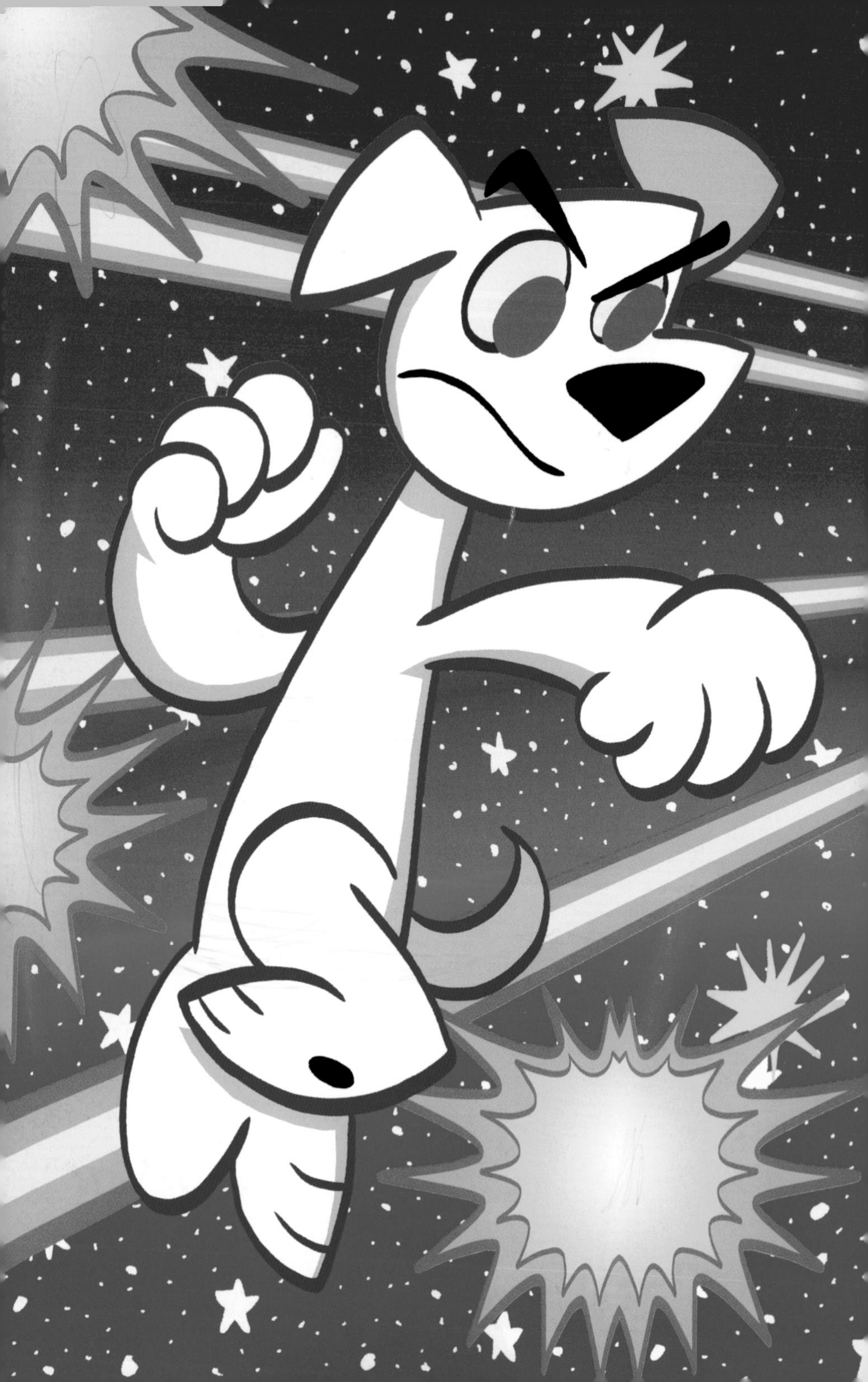

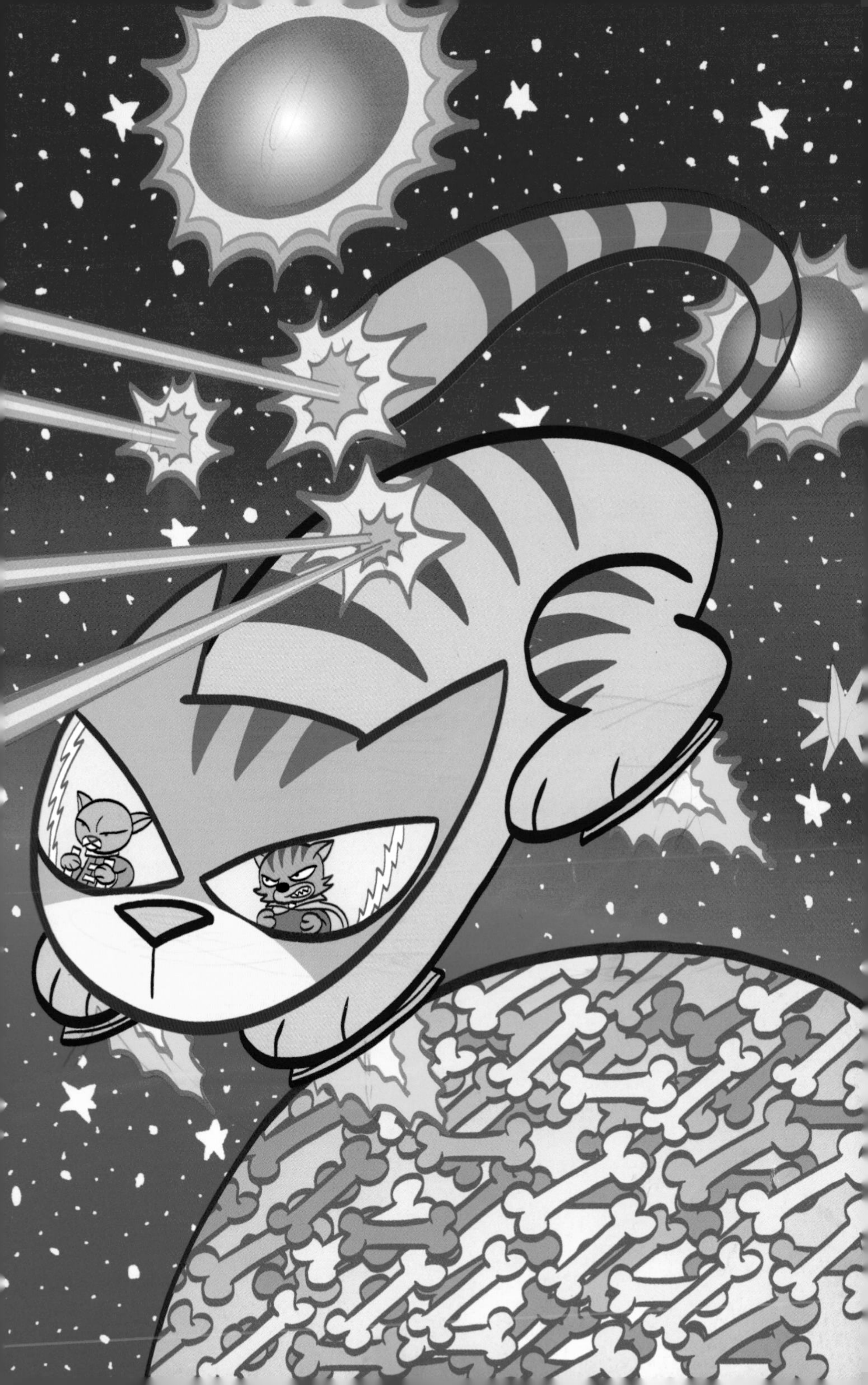

When the smoke cleared, the
giggling cats looked out the windows.
They were astonished to see Krypto
flying through the air, heading right at
their spaceship!

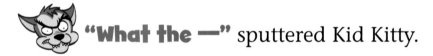 **"What the —"** sputtered Kid Kitty.

**"They don't call me the Dog of
Steel for nothing!"** yelled Krypto.

Krypto used his super-strong jaws
to tear a giant hole in the side of the
spaceship.

"ACK!" cried the Cat Crime Club

members. They tumbled from the ship

and landed on the planet with a thud.

Suddenly, Tail Terrier stepped out

from behind the pile of bones. The

other members of the S.C.P.A. followed.

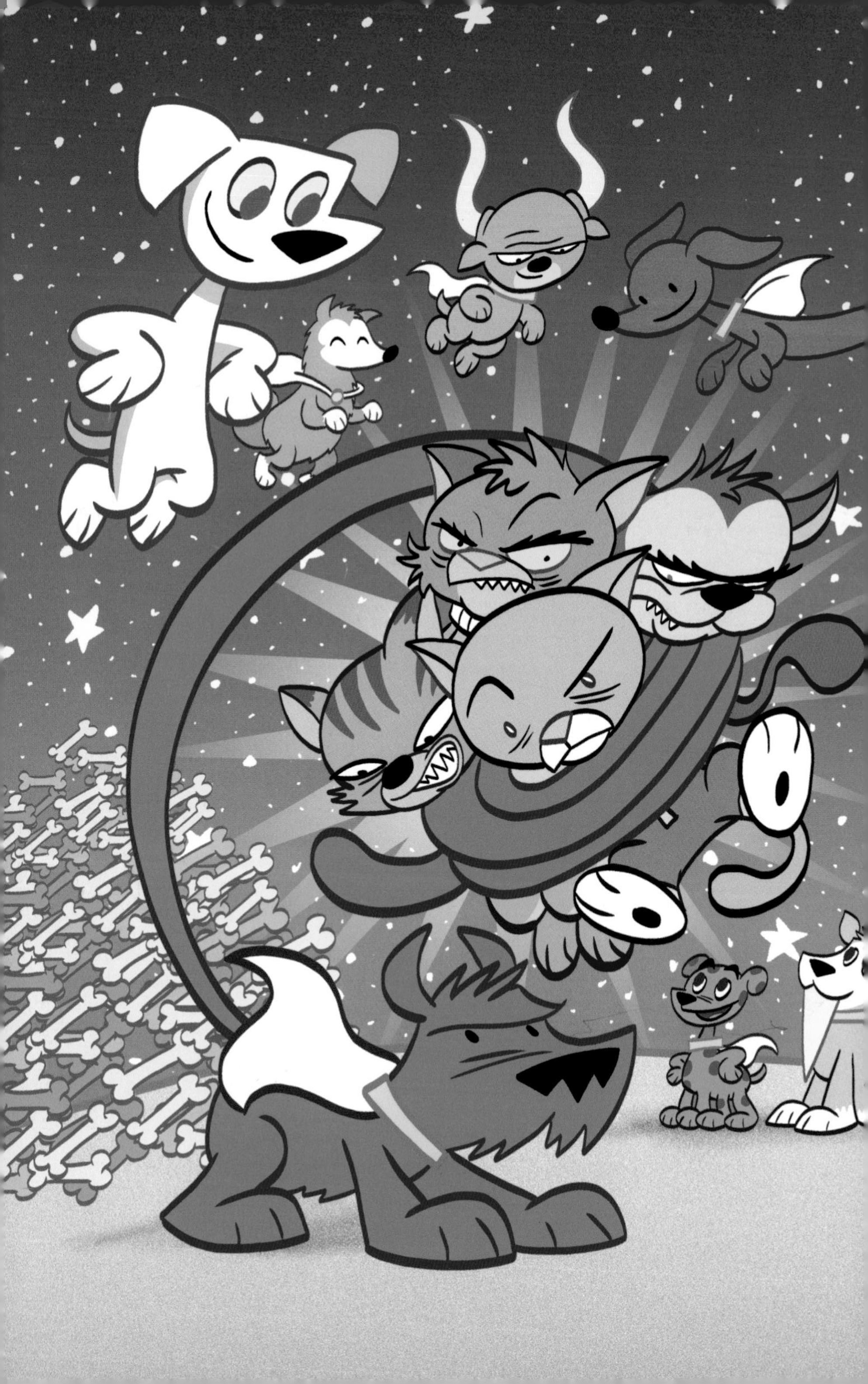

The pooches had known their friend Krypto would save the day. Tail Terrier used his tail to bind the angry cats together so they couldn't squirm away.

"Why didn't the red suns affect Krypto's powers?" asked Purring Pete.

"It was because they weren't red suns at all," Krypto said. "Before you arrived, I grabbed two red lava discs from a nearby volcano. I kicked them into orbit in front of the planet's two yellow suns. That gave the appearance of two red suns!"

Hissing and spitting, the Cat Crime Club admitted defeat. The feline felons even agreed to return the stolen money from the All-Paws Circus.

Krypto was a hero!

Back at the Space Canine Patrol Agency headquarters, the Super-Dog got back his collar and cape. He joyously led his fellow canines in saying their oath:

"Big dog! Big dog! Bow, wow, wow! We'll crush evil! Now, now, now!"

With their tails wagging, the

members of the S.C.P.A. waved farewell

to Krypto. The Super-Dog zoomed up,

up, and away and headed home.

WHOOSH!

Two days had passed since he started playing fetch with Superman. As soon as Krypto reached Earth, he was surprised to see that Superman was holding the giant steel rod that he had thrown into outer space.

"I had to retrieve this myself, Krypto," said Superman. "Where have you been for the past two days, old pal? Did you get sleepy and take a catnap?"

"Woof! Woof!" Krypto smiled and nodded. *Close enough,* he thought.

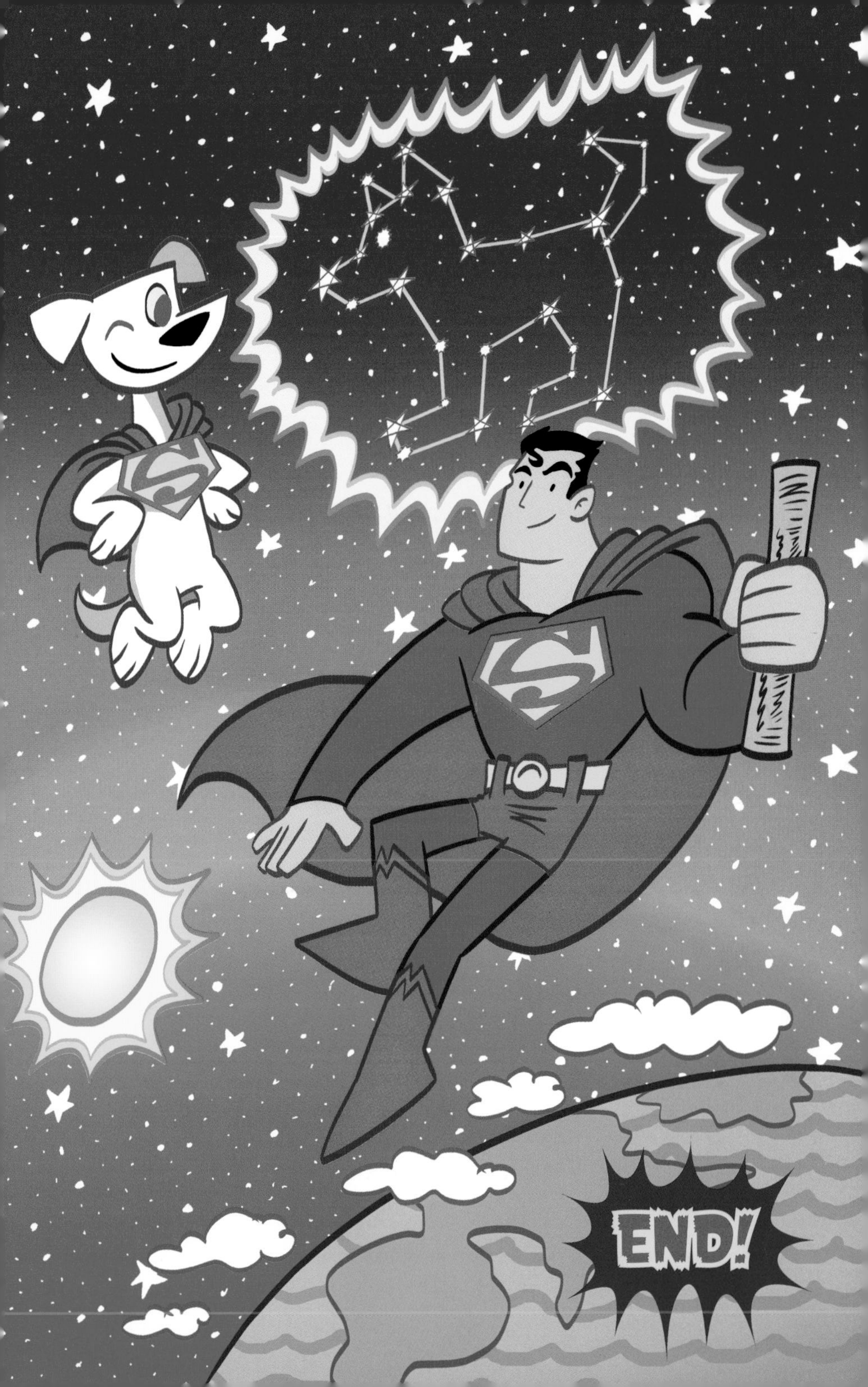
END!

KNOW YOUR HERO PETS!

1. Krypto
2. Streaky
3. Whizzy
4. Comet
5. Beppo
6. Super-Turtle
7. Fuzzy
8. Ace
9. Robin Robin
10. Batcow
11. Jumpa
12. Whatzit
13. Hoppy
14. Tawky Tawny
15. Spot
16. Plastic Frog
17. Gleek
18. Big Ted
19. Dawg
20. Space Dolphins
21. Proty
22. Chameleon Collie
23. Bull Dog
24. Paw Pooch
25. Tusky Husky
26. Hot Dog
27. Tail Terrier
28. Mammoth Mutt
29. Prophetic Pup
30. Rex the Wonder Dog
31. Detective Chimp
32. Starlene
33. Mossy
34. Merle
35. Loafers
36. Storm
37. Topo
38. Ark
39. Fluffy
40. Betty
41. Geoffrey
42. B'dg
43. Sen-Tag
44. Fendor
45. Stripezoid
46. Zallion
47. Ribitz
48. Bzzd
49. Gratch
50. Buzzoo
51. Fossfur
52. Zhoomp
53. Eeny

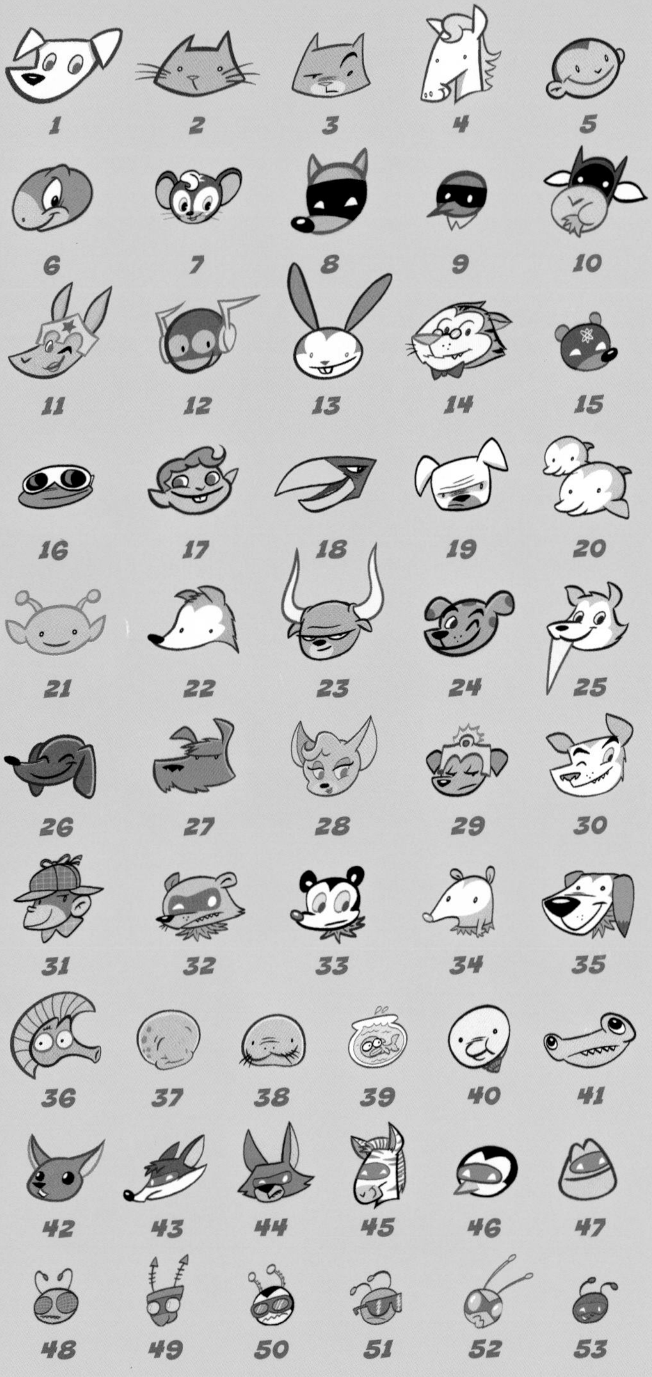
1 2 3 4 5
6 7 8 9 10
11 12 13 14 15
16 17 18 19 20
21 22 23 24 25
26 27 28 29 30
31 32 33 34 35
36 37 38 39 40 41
42 43 44 45 46 47
48 49 50 51 52 53

KNOW YOUR VILLAIN PETS!

1. Bizarro Krypto
2. Ignatius
3. Brainicat
4. Mechanikat
5. Dogwood
6. General Manx
7. Nizz
8. Fer-El
9. Crackers
10. Giggles
11. Artie Puffin
12. Griff
13. Waddles
14. Rozz
15. Mad Catter
16. Croward
17. Chauncey
18. Bit-Bit & X-43
19. Dr. Spider
20. Anna Conda
21. Mr. Mind
22. Sobek
23. Patches
24. Dex-Starr
25. Glomulus
26. Titano
27. Purring Pete
28. Kid Kitty
29. Scratchy Tom
30. Gat-Cat
31. Starro
32. Mama Ripples
33. Faye Precious
34. Limpy
35. Offie Lee
36. Misty
37. Sneezers
38. Johnny
39. Joey
40. Frankie
41. George
42. Whoosh
43. Pronto
44. Snorrt
45. Rolf
46. Squealer
47. Kajunn
48. Tootz
49. Eezix
50. Donald
51. Waxxee
52. Fimble
53. Webbik

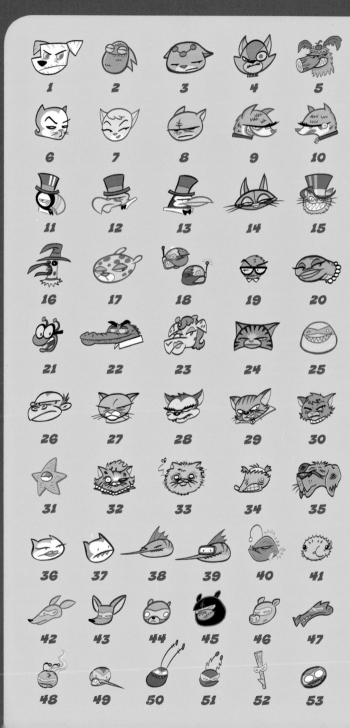

MEET THE AUTHOR!

Steve Korté

Steve Korté is a freelance writer. At DC Comics he edited over 500 books. Among the titles he edited are *75 Years of DC Comics*, winner of the 2011 Eisner Award, and *Jack Cole and Plastic Man*, winner of the 2002 Harvey Award. He lives in New York City with his own super-cat Duke.

MEET THE ILLUSTRATOR!

Eisner Award-winner Art Baltazar

Art Baltazar is a cartoonist machine from the heart of Chicago! He defines cartoons and comics not only as an art style, but as a way of life. Currently, Art is the creative force behind *The New York Times* best-selling, Eisner Award-winning, DC Comics series Tiny Titans, and the co-writer for *Billy Batson and the Magic of SHAZAM!* Art is living the dream! He draws comics and never has to leave the house. He lives with his lovely wife, Rose, big boy Sonny, little boy Gordon, and little girl Audrey. Right on!

WORD POWER!

asteroid (ASS-tur-roid)—one of thousands of rocks, or minor planets, that travel around the sun

elastic (i-LASS-tik)— capable of returning to original shape after being stretched, pressed, or squeezed together

galaxy (GAL-uhk-see)—a very large group of stars and planets

geyser (GYE-zur)—a hole in the ground through which hot water and steam shoot up in bursts

headquarters (HED-kwor-turz)—the place from which an organization is run

Kryptonite (KRIHP-tuh-nite)—a radioactive rock from the planet Krypton

meteorite (MEE-tee-ur-rite)—a piece of a meteor that falls to earth before it has burned up

oath (OHTH)—a serious, formal promise

AW YEAH!

ART BALTAZAR
SAYS:

**HERO DOGS
GALORE!**

**SPACE CANINE
PATROL AGENCY!**

**KRYPTO THE
SUPER-DOG!**

BATCOW!

**FLUFFY AND THE
AQUA-PETS!**

**PLASTIC
FROG!**

**JUMPA
THE KANGA!**

**STORM AND THE
AQUA-PETS!**

**STREAKY
THE SUPER-CAT!**

**THE TERRIFIC
WHATZIT!**

SUPER-TURTLE!

**BIG TED
AND DAWG!**

Read all of these totally awesome stories today, starring all of your favorite DC SUPER-PETS!

GREEN LANTERN BUG CORPS!

SPOT!

ROBIN ROBIN AND ACE TEAM-UP!

SPACE CANINE PATROL AGENCY!

HOPPY!

BEPPO THE SUPER-MONKEY!

ACE THE BAT-HOUND!

KRYPTO AND ACE TEAM-UP!

B'DG, THE GREEN LANTERN!

THE LEGION OF SUPER-PETS!

COMET THE SUPER-HORSE!

DOWN HOME CRITTER GANG!

THE FUN DOESN'T STOP HERE!

Discover more:

- Videos & Contests!
- Games & Puzzles!
- Heroes & Villains!
- Authors & Illustrators!

@ www.capstonekids.com

Find cool websites and more books like this one at www.facthound.com Just type in Book I.D. 9781404864931 and you're ready to go!

⊞ Picture Window Books™

Published in 2012
A Capstone Imprint
1710 Roe Crest Drive
North Mankato, MN 56003
www.capstonepub.com

Copyright © 2012 DC Comics.
All related characters and elements are trademarks
of and © DC Comics.
(s12)

STAR26103

All rights reserved. No part of this publication may
be reproduced in whole or in part, or stored in a
retrieval system, or transmitted in any form or by
any means, electronic, mechanical, photocopying,
recording, or otherwise, without written permission.

Cataloging-in-Publication Data is available at
the Library of Congress website.
ISBN: 978-1-4048-6493-1 (library binding)
ISBN: 978-1-4048-7665-1 (paperback)

Summary: The evil Cat Crime Club is on the
prowl at a local circus. Luckily, the Space
Canine Patrol Agents are standing guard.
But when their leader, Krypto the Super-Dog,
can't stop these feline felons, he's in the team's
doghouse. To win back their trust, Krypto must
prove he's still the pride of the pack.

Art Director & Designer: Bob Lentz
Editor: Donald Lemke
Creative Director: Heather Kindseth
Editorial Director: Michael Dahl

Printed in the United States of America
in Stevens Point, Wisconsin.
032012   006678WZF12

DC™

SUPER-PETS!

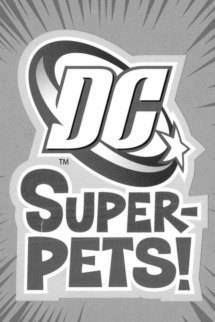

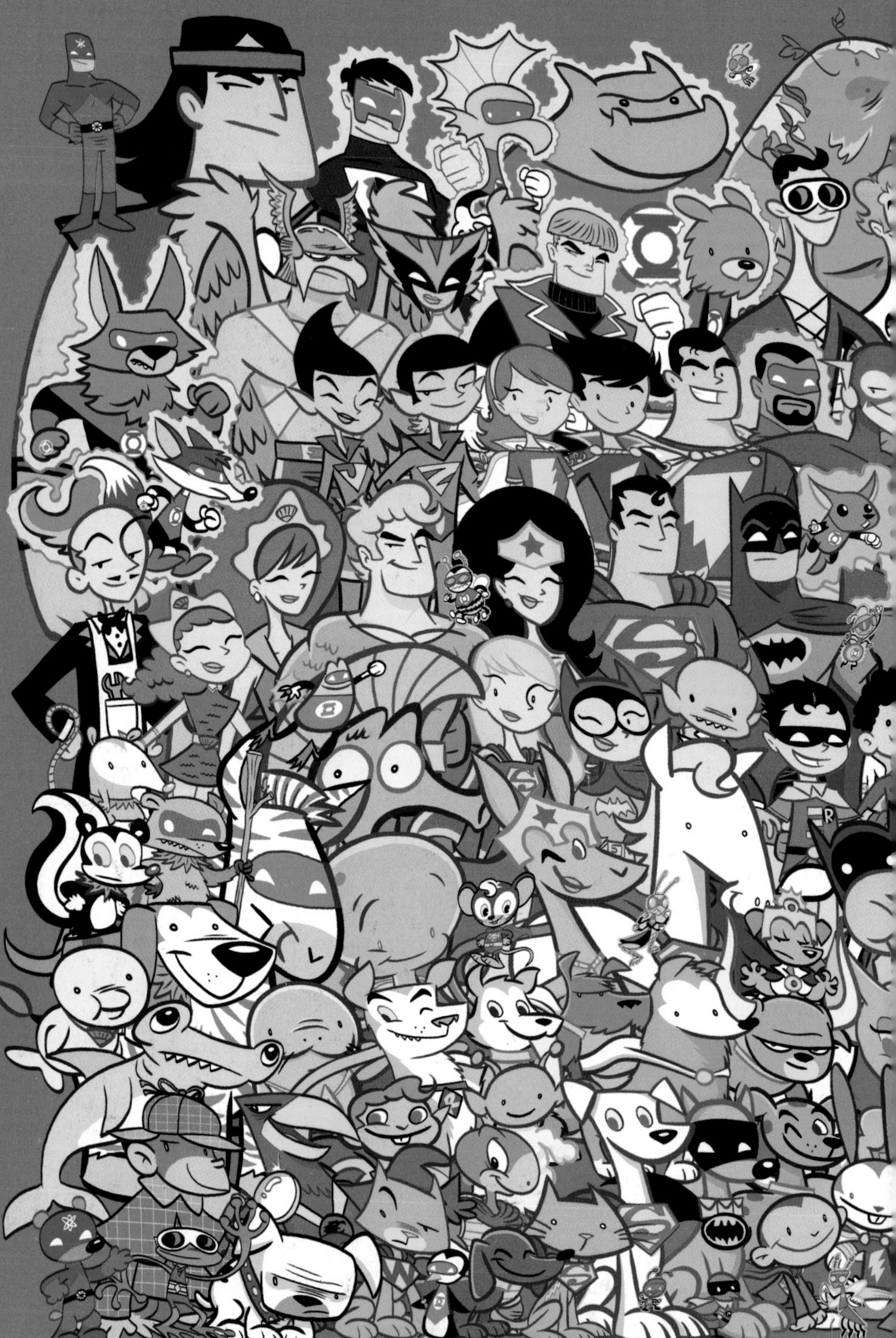